THE
CLASSIC

TURBOC

HARGED

THE
CLASSIC
'69 CHEVY CAMARO

Eric Stevens

MINNEAPOLIS

Darby Creek
A division of Lerner Publishing Group, Inc.
241 First Avenue North
Minneapolis, MN 55401 U.S.A.

Website address: www.lernerbooks.com

The images in this book are used with the permisison of:
Cover and interior photograph © iStockphoto.com/Ken Babione.

Main body text set in Janson Text LT Std 12/17.
Typeface provided by Linotype AG.

Library of Congress Cataloging-in-Publication Data

Stevens, Eric, 1974–
    The classic : '69 Chevy Camaro / by Eric Stevens.
        pages cm. — (Turbocharged)
    ISBN 978–1–4677–1247–7 (lib. bdg. : alk. paper)
    ISBN 978–1–4677–1671–0 (eBook)
    [1. Muscle cars—Fiction. 2. Fathers and sons—Fiction. 3. Automobile
racing—Fiction.] I. Title.
PZ7.S84443Cl 2013
    [Fic]—dc23   2013002930

Manufactured in the United States of America
1 – BP – 7/15/13

CHAPTER ONE

Eddie King, rookie driver, kept his eyes on the length of perfectly smooth asphalt before him. He could see the heat of the late summer day coming off the blackness in waves.

The starting lights flashed amber. Eddie revved the engine and adjusted his grip on the four-speed shifter of his Camaro SS.

A classic. One of the most sought-after American muscle cars.

The green light lit up. Eddie pulled off the clutch and floored the heavy gas pedal, lurching from the line. His 430 horsepower engine growled ferociously.

The RPMs screamed up to near 7,000, and Eddie shifted into second. He'd already left his opponent in the dust. No match for the Camaro's massive 427 cubic inch engine.

With a final roar at well over a hundred miles per hour, the Camaro blasted across the quarter-mile line. Under twelve seconds.

"Yes," whispered Eddie, a triumphant grin on his face. He downshifted and pulled onto the side of the road.

✳ ✳ ✳

"So. How'd I do?"

Eddie switched off the little blue four-door Kia and pulled out the key.

The examiner, a stodgy woman in her fifties, clucked her tongue and ticked down the list of items on her clipboard. "A point off for butchering the parallel park," she said. "And another for the tire squeal on the left turn onto Washington."

She looked at him with a cruel glimmer in

her eyes. "You took that turn too fast."

Eddie swallowed and tried to get a look at the clipboard, but the examiner blocked it with her shoulder.

"Lucky for you," the examiner said, looking back at her list, "those were your only two red marks."

Eddie gasped. "So I pass?" he said.

The examiner sighed and said, "Yes. Congratulations."

"I can't believe it!" Eddie said to his mom on the bus ride home. "I have a driver's license."

She smiled at him as she slipped her bus pass back into her purse. "I wish we could afford to get you a car," she said. "Even a used one."

Eddie shrugged, still grinning. "I've got my job," he said. "I've been saving. I'll be able to buy something eventually."

His mom smiled at him, but he could tell she wasn't so sure. A moment later, the bus's loud brakes shrieked as it pulled up in front of the downtown hospital.

"Here's me," Mom said. She gave Eddie's cheek a quick kiss.

After she got up, Eddie sagged in his seat and watched her climb off the bus and step inside the hospital for her shift. He leaned his head on the window and thought about the classic muscle car—the one he'd daydreamed about during his driving exam—rusting away under a tarp in their backyard.

CHAPTER TWO

Eddie sat on the back stoop of his little house on the north side of the city and looked out over the tiny brown yard. The Camaro—his dad's old car—had been there, covered with a tarp, for as long as Eddie could remember.

"If I ever get a weekend off," Dad used to say, "I'll get to work on that hunk of junk."

Mom would come up next to him while Eddie played in the plastic sandbox not far from the old car.

"We ought to sell it for scrap," she said one

morning, slipping an arm around Dad's waist. "Might get fifty bucks for it. We could eat for a month."

Dad grunted and pulled away. Eddie was only a little kid at the time—not even five—but he remembered it like it was yesterday. He remembered how the sun coming over the house caught his eye and made him squint.

He remembered Dad pulling open the screen door like he was mad at it. He remembered how Mom's shoulders shook as the screen door slammed closed, like it always did.

Mom smiled at him after a moment. "We sure have to get that door fixed," she said. Then she followed Dad inside.

Dad had been gone for nine years now. He walked out a couple of days before Eddie's seventh birthday. Eddie had hardly seen or heard from him since.

Today, holding his brand-new temporary license—a yellow, fragile-looking piece of paper with loads of fine print all over it—

Eddie wondered why Mom still hadn't sold the car for scrap.

Eddie stood up from the back stoop and walked over to the Camaro. He pulled off the heavy gray tarp. Underneath, in desperate need of a paint job and who knows what kind of work under the hood, was the 1969 Camaro SS. The car his dad had worked so hard to buy when he'd been in high school.

In the low light of the late afternoon, it actually looked pretty awesome. Eddie could imagine his dad at Eddie's age, sitting in the driver's seat, revving the monstrous engine. It might have been how he first got Mom's attention.

Gross.

I've been working hard too, Eddie thought to himself, walking around the old car. *I've been saving for my own car.*

He leaned on the driver's side door. *But why should I wait?* he thought, a smile growing on his face. *I could use my savings to fix up the Camaro.*

With a grin a mile wide, Eddie ran inside

to call Mom at work. She'd probably be
thrilled with the idea.

CHAPTER THREE

The next morning, Eddie popped the Camaro's hood and stared at the engine. He knew it was a 427 cubic inch big block—his dad had said so many times. Plus, Eddie had done some reading online—now and then during computer class in school, usually when he was supposed to be doing something else.

But knowing the Camaro's specs didn't make him an expert in getting the old thing running again. With one hand on the opened hood lid and the other on his hip, Eddie sighed.

"This won't be so easy, huh?" his mom said. She came up next to him, her huge mug of tea in both hands.

"I can do it," Eddie said, avoiding eye contact as he dropped the hood onto the dusty, rusty engine. "If Dad could do it, I can too."

Mom raised her eyebrows.

Eddie headed for the house. "I gotta get ready for school," he said.

"Your father worked on cars his whole life," Mom said, following him inside. "Heck, he knew that car inside and out. He turned every bolt himself, he used to brag."

Eddie pulled a toaster pastry from the box and unwrapped it. He glared at his mother as she leaned on the counter, smiling.

"You know, he bought that Camaro for almost nothing," she said with a faraway look in her eyes.

Eddie could never guess how Mom would act when the subject of Dad came up. Sometimes she'd lash out and snap at whoever was around—usually Eddie. But sometimes she got that dreamy look and a goofy smile, like she actually missed the guy.

She took a loud sip of her tea, the steam from the cup fogging her glasses—she only wore them in the morning, before switching them out for contacts.

"It didn't run then," she said. "Wouldn't even start up. But he got it running—and running like a stallion too. Kept it running till—well, right around when you were born, I guess. Then work got in the way."

"I know, Mom," Eddie said. "So maybe I can get it running too. Did you think of that?"

"Of course," she said, patting his shoulder. Eddie groaned. "But it won't happen overnight."

She put down her tea and checked the phone on the stove. With a gasp, she hurried to the bathroom. "I gotta get going!" she said, closing the bathroom door. "I'll be late."

Eddie dumped Mom's tea and rinsed the cup. He leaned on the sink and thought about his dad.

"I haven't seen him in years," he muttered. "He won't even recognize me."

Eddie grabbed his backpack and called out, "Bye, Mom. Off to school."

Then he was out the door, heading for the city bus. Before it even pulled up, he'd made up his mind. If that's what it would take to get the Camaro running again, then after school that day, he'd track down dear old Dad.

CHAPTER FOUR

Eddie couldn't exactly ask Mom. He wasn't that dumb. If he did, she'd try to talk him out of it, for one thing. And she probably wouldn't tell him where to find Dad anyway—if she even knew.

Eddie had one hope for tracking the old man down without Mom's help. He headed straight from school to the pharmacy on the other side of Lake Street. The little bell over the door rang when he stepped inside.

It was cluttered and small, smelling of dust and floor cleaner and mouthwash, just like he remembered it. Right near the entrance stood two old arcade driving games. Beside them stood the little plastic stool he used to stand on to play when he was too small to reach the steering wheels.

"Looking for anything in particular?" said the old woman behind the counter. Eddie struggled to remember her name, but it was just out of reach. She had been old when he was a little kid, and she was still old.

"Um," said Eddie.

She gave him a nasty look, twisting up her lips in distaste.

She probably hates teenagers, Eddie thought. *She probably thinks I'm in here trying to score cigarettes or condoms or something.*

"I'm . . ." Eddie started to say. "I'm fine, thanks."

He headed up the center aisle, where the old lady wouldn't be able to watch him. Eddie scanned the shelf as he walked: aspirin, cold medicine, antacids, suppositories. He wasn't watching where he was going, and he nearly tripped over the old guy kneeling in the aisle.

"Sorry," Eddie said, grabbing the shelves for balance and nearly taking down an entire display of pregnancy tests.

"That's all right," the old man said as he looked up. He stopped short. "Well, I'll be," he said, staring at Eddie.

Eddie looked away. "What?" he said.

The old man shook his head and laughed. "I swear, I thought I'd gone back in time," he said. With a groan, he stood up. "You look like somebody who worked for me—oh, five or eight years ago."

"Oh," Eddie said, looking at his feet.

"But you can't be more than fifteen," the man added.

"Sixteen," Eddie said. "Listen—"

The man wasn't listening. He shook his head and laughed, his eyes closed tight. "I wonder whatever became of him. Had a family, I think."

Eddie's sighed. "Then you don't know," he mumbled.

"What's that?" the old man said.

Eddie shook his head. "Never mind," he

said. "I was hoping my dad still worked here, but—"

The old man's eyes went wide, and Eddie recognized him: he was Mr. Tuft, the shop's owner. And the old lady at the counter was his wife.

"Then you're little Eddie King," he said. He pointed toward the front and added, "You used to stand up there and drive those video game cars for hours while your dad stocked the shelves and your mom got her hair done next door."

"Yup," Eddie said. "That's me. I'm, um, looking for him. For my dad."

Mr. Tuft's face went stern and cold. He nodded once, sharply. "I see," he said. He put a strong, wrinkled hand on Eddie's shoulder. "Suzie," he called out—*that* was her name. "Get a Coke for Eddie, all right?"

"That's okay," Eddie said, but Mr. Tuft waved him off like it was no big deal. Mrs. Tuft delivered Eddie an open can of Coke.

"Last I heard from your dad," the old man, "he'd got in a little trouble."

"Like, police?" Eddie asked. He took a sip from the Coke.

Mr. Tuft nodded. "It didn't sound like anything too serious. I don't think he went to jail. He was just mixed up with a bad crew. I had to let him go."

"What did he do?" Eddie said.

The old man reached down into the box he'd been unloading and pulled out two huge bottles of aspirin. "Drag racing," he said, his voice deep and rough. He obviously didn't approve of Dad's favorite pastime. "It's all he ever talked about."

"Ah," Eddie said, thinking about the Camaro in the backyard.

Mr. Tuft shook a bottle of aspirin in Eddie's face. "I warned him all the time!" he snarled over the rattling of pills. "But did he listen? Bah!"

"Well," Eddie said, "do you know where I can find him?"

Mr. Tuft coughed and put the bottles on the shelf with the others. "Who knows," he said. With more vigor than he appeared to have at first glance, Mr. Tuft scooped up the empty crate and hauled it toward the back of the store.

"Great," Eddie muttered, and he turned to leave. Instead, he walked right into Mrs. Tuft, who'd been listening nearby.

"You seem like a nice kid," she said quietly. "And I don't blame you for wanting to find your dad, even if he is up to no good now and then."

"You know where he is?" Eddie asked.

"Well, not exactly," the old woman said. "But I know where he might be found."

CHAPTER FIVE

There were no drag strips in the city limits.
They took up a lot of room. They reeked of
oil and fuel and exhaust. And they sent up a
racket like all the demons of hell storming
through its open gates.

To Eddie, it sounded like heaven. But
to the city planners, it must have sounded
pretty bad. That meant to get to the nearest
track with a drag strip, Eddie had to catch
a bus out to the western suburbs. The ride
took over an hour and a half, and that didn't
include the half-hour walk from the bus stop

to the track.

When Eddie got there, he checked the schedule and sighed with relief. Old Mrs. Tuft's tip was right: it was Grudge Night. Dozens of amateur drivers with their street-legal cars would be taking pass after pass. According to Mrs. Tuft, Eddie might find his dad among them.

General admission was five bucks. Eddie paid up and went in among the crowds. They all shouted loudly, some in cool-looking driver's uniforms but most in jeans and shirts. They showed off stats and tickets—slips that showed their times on the track.

Down at the track and all over the sidelines, guys and a couple of girls stood next to hot rods and classics and a few show cars and funny cars. The cars' hoods were popped open, their engines gleaming or chugging and roaring. The proud owners showed off their specs and customizations, bragging about horsepower and pass times.

Eddie walked among the drivers and owners, checking out faces and sneaking glances under low-brimmed caps. Even though Eddie hadn't seen his dad in almost ten years, he remembered him well enough. None of these guys were him.

"The old lady was wrong," he muttered to himself, ready to give up and grab the bus for home. "Mom will be worrying where I am, anyway."

But on his way to the exit, he spotted a smaller group of young men in the stands. On a Grudge Night, the stands weren't full of spectators like they would be for an official NHRA event or something. Mostly, it was the friends and family of the guys showing off on the strip.

This group, though, was gathered together near the fence, looking at programs and passing cash around. One of them, his back to Eddie, had a very familiar way of standing.

Eddie hurried to the stands, up and over the bridge from the infield and down the bleachers. His tennis shoes clonked on the metal steps.

Hardly slowing down, he headed over to

the group of guys by the fence. The face of
the man with the familiar stance was hidden
under the low, flat brim of his baseball cap. He
was counting out cash.

"Twenty, forty, sixty," he said, shuffling
through the bills, some crisp and some old and
sad-looking. He handed the stack to another
guy in the circle. "There. Two hundred.
Congrats, Lefty. You win again."

Eddie moved in closer as the man who'd
lost the bet lifted his head.

"Dad?" Eddie said.

The other men in the circle backed up and
widened the group.

"Uh," said the man in the baseball cap.
He shoved his billfold into the pocket of his
jeans. The other men turned to watch him,
wondering if this could be true—if this boy
could really be his son.

He smiled. His voice cracked as he said,
"Eddie. What are you doing here?"

"Then it is you," Eddie said. He couldn't
help smiling too.

"You guys excuse us, all right?" his dad

said to the others. The circle dissolved, the other men moving farther along the fence.

"Look at you," Dad said, sitting down on the metal bleachers.

Eddie leaned on the fence and looked down at himself. He wasn't sure what he was supposed to be seeing, but Dad laughed.

"I mean it's been ten years," he said.

"Eight," Eddie corrected him.

"The point is you're huge now. Man."

"I guess," Eddie said. "Um, are you driving tonight?"

Dad's eyes went wide. "Drive? Me?" he said. "No way. These guys spend every penny on their cars. I hardly have two pennies to rub together, after rent and food and child supp—"

He stopped short and stood up, chuckling. "I don't even have my own car, Eddie," he said. "I take the bus out here a few nights a week to keep up with the scene, lose a few bets . . ."

"Oh," Eddie said. He looked at his feet.

"Listen, it's cool to see you," his dad said. "Funny running into you like this. I guess you're into drag racing now too, huh?"

"What?" Dad thought this was a coincidence, Eddie realized. He didn't figure that Eddie had come out to the track especially to find him. "Um, yeah. That's right. Actually, I was thinking about fixing up the old Camaro."

Dad's face lit up. "Ah, that old beast," he said. "Man, if I had that thing running like ten years ago, I'd be out here every Thursday night. On the *other* side of this fence."

Eddie laughed. "Well, I have my license now," he said. "I figured if I get it running again, I could use it. You know, sometimes. Might be cool."

"You should've seen it when I was your age," Dad said. "Or a little older, I guess. We'd hit the freeway and race the straightaways. Man, no one could keep up with the Camaro."

"Mom says you know every bolt on that car," Eddie said.

"Damn straight," Dad said.

"So I was wondering," Eddie went on, "will you help me rebuild it?"

Dad's smile grew. He clapped a hand on Eddie's shoulder. "For sure," he said. "That sounds amazing."

CHAPTER SIX

Dad wouldn't come by until Mom was off to work.

"Sorry about this," Dad said as he dropped his coat over the back fence and pushed up his sleeves. "You'll understand when you're older."

Eddie shrugged. He was pretty sure he understood already.

Dad opened the driver's side door and climbed in. His grin grew 1,000 percent as he put both hands on the steering wheel and looked out over the hood—even if it was in desperate need of a paint job. Eddie stood in front of the car. For an instant, he thought his dad was grinning at him.

"Brings back memories," Dad said. He sighed, then reached down and popped the hood. "Let's see what we're dealing with."

He climbed out and joined Eddie at the grill. Together, they leaned over the engine.

✳ ✳ ✳

A few hours later, everything under the hood was out of the car and laid on a tarp on the lawn. Dad stepped back from the Camaro, wiping his greasy hands on a rag.

"Now what?" Eddie said.

"Parts store," Dad said. He put an arm around Eddie's shoulders, and Eddie grinned. It was good to have Dad back. "Still one up on the avenue?"

"Yeah," Eddie said. "We can walk."

"Great," said dad, grabbing his coat off the fence. "Hey, listen. You have a little cash, right?"

"Sure," Eddie said. "I've been saving up for my own car, so I figure fixing up the Camaro is even better."

"Great," Dad said. "Lost a few hundred bucks last night."

"It's fine," Eddie said. The two of them headed up the street to the parts store. It turned out Eddie had enough for the small parts—new gaskets and seals, O-rings, clamps, bolts and nuts, a new V-belt. Cheap stuff.

"This might hurt," Dad said. He held open the parts catalog—a huge, battered book. He dropped his finger on a gleaming piece of machinery: the carburetor for a 427 cubic inch 1969 Camaro motor.

Eddie checked the price. "Whoa," he said.

"I know," Dad said.

"Can't we just repair the carb?" Eddie said. "Rebuild, clean it up?"

"Nah," Dad said, closing the book and dropping it on the bright yellow counter. "Castings are cracked. The carb is shot."

"How about a junkyard?" Eddie tried.

"Must be cheaper than new, right?"

"The 1969 Camaro is a very special car," Dad said. "Especially mine, with that 450 horsepower big block. They're expensive to find new—and nearly impossible to find original."

Eddie took a deep breath and let his shoulders sag. "I don't have enough money," he said. "Sorry to waste your time."

"Man, don't be ridiculous," Dad said, patting Eddie on the back. "We'll get the new carb, no problem."

"How?" Eddie said.

"I don't have cash on me right now," Dad said, "but I can get it. I'll make sure we get what we need to get that beast running again, all right?"

Eddie smiled. "Thanks," he said. He paid for the other parts—the cheap stuff—and they headed home.

CHAPTER SEVEN

The next day was Sunday, but Mom didn't get the day off. She hadn't been gone more than a few minutes when a car pulled up in front of the house. Eddie hurried outside when he saw his dad climb out of the passenger seat.

"Hey, man," Dad called from the curb. He went to the trunk as the driver popped it open. "Got a little surprise in there. Gimme a hand."

Eddie jogged to his side as the trunk lid lifted up.

"Ta-dah," said Dad, and there it was: the carburetor.

"Wow!" Eddie said. "How'd you get it?"

Eddie's dad lifted the thing out of the trunk and handed it to Eddie. With a free hand, Dad slammed the lid down and called to the driver, "Thanks a lot, Reggie. See you later."

They carried the carburetor around to the back.

"So?" Eddie said. "How'd you come up with the cash so quick?"

"Don't worry about that," Dad said. "The point is we got it. And this Camaro will be running before the week's out."

"Awesome," Eddie said, grinning. They set the carburetor on the tarp with the rest of the parts. Eddie stood over the parts. It looked like a lot of work, getting this car put back together. But he couldn't take his eyes off the carburetor.

It was spotless—brand new. A $700 part. And Eddie had no clue how his dad had come up with the money to get it so quickly.

And on a Sunday morning. Something didn't seem right. Eddie tried to think of how to ask, but he knew what it would sound like if he did: an accusation. So instead of bringing it up, he rolled up his sleeves and got down to business.

By the time Mom was due home, there was still plenty of work to do. "We made great progress, though," Dad said. He mussed Eddie's hair. "Man, I can't get over it. You're learning quick too."

"Thanks," Eddie said.

"Just like your dad, am I right?" Dad said, laughing. He checked the time on his phone. "I better go grab the bus now, though. Your mom will be home any minute, right?"

"I guess," Eddie said. "You can stick around and say hey if you want. I don't think she'd mind."

"I better not," Dad said, pulling on his coat. "Like I said: you'll understand when you're older."

"Right," Eddie said.

Dad zipped his coat and said, "Walk me to the bus stop, all right?"

"Why?" Eddie said.

"Gotta talk to you about something," Dad said. They headed around front and started up the block toward the white and blue bus stop sign. It wasn't far.

"What's up?" Eddie said.

"I can tell you're weirded out about the new carb," Dad said. "And you probably know I haven't always been on the right side of the law, as the saying goes."

Eddie had been thinking exactly that, but he didn't want to say so. He just shrugged instead. Dad clapped him on the back twice.

"Well don't even worry about that," Dad said. "I might not be a model citizen, but I haven't been in trouble in a real long time, okay?"

"Okay," Eddie said.

"I had a little money stored away," Dad said. "And I figured, what better way to spend it than on the old Camaro? She means an awful lot to me."

She does? Eddie thought. *What about me?*

"Anyway, thanks for walking with me," Dad said as they reached the bus stop. He nodded toward Eddie's house. "I see your mom walking up. You better get back."

"Okay," Eddie said. "Um, you know when can you come out again? We still have a lot to do."

"Not sure, man," Dad said. "I'll talk to you tomorrow, all right?"

✳ ✳ ✳

At home, Eddie found Mom in the kitchen going through the mail, her coat still on and her bag still hanging from her arm.

"Hey," Eddie said.

"The Camaro's looking in pretty good shape," she said without lifting her eyes off the mail. "How's Dad?"

Eddie's jaw dropped. "Uhh . . . What?"

Mom smirked. "It's okay, Ed," she said. "You're allowed to see him. He is your father."

"Oh," Eddie said. "I mean, I didn't mean to hide it from you or anything. It just sort of—I don't know."

She put down the mail and exhaled slowly.

When she turned to face Eddie, a small smile was forming on her face. "How is he?" she said. "Really."

Eddie shrugged. "Fine, I guess," he said. Then he brightened, thinking of the brand-new carburetor they'd installed. "He's really helping with the Camaro. We think it'll be running this week."

"That's great," Mom said. "It'll need a paint job too, I think."

She stood there for a few seconds, leaning on the counter. Then she groaned. "Such a long day. I need a shower."

CHAPTER EIGHT

At school the next day, Eddie was heading for his normal lunch table when he walked past a group of kids from the auto tech school.

"I'll probably run my Cougar," said one guy with a little roll of one shoulder, like it was no big deal. "It's doing the quarter mile in 10.3."

Even Eddie knew that probably wasn't true, but he didn't say anything. He did, however, sit at the nearest table to listen in.

"You can't put that thing in the show, though," said another kid as he flipped through some car magazine. "It looks like garbage."

"Shut it," the first kid said.

A third guy laughed. "He's right. And even if you could run a ten-second quarter-mile pass—which we all know you can't—you'd lose so many points on the show that my Mustang would beat you if I pushed it for the quarter mile."

That got the whole table laughing. Eddie took the opportunity to lean over and ask, "Hey, what are you guys talking about? A classic car show?"

"A drag race and show," said one of the guys after glancing at the others. They didn't know Eddie, and the auto tech kids tended to stick together. "It's next weekend."

"Can anyone enter?" Eddie said.

The guys snickered into their hands.

"I guess," said the motorhead. "Why, you got a cherry little classic car lying around?"

"A 1969 Camaro SS," Eddie said. "450 horsepower."

One of the auto tech guys whistled. They

were definitely impressed.

"Yeah, you can enter," said the first guy. "Sign-ups at the shop door."

Eddie nodded and turned back to his lunch.

※ ※ ※

The minute Eddie walked in after school, he picked up the phone and called his Dad. If the Camaro was going to be race-and-show ready by the weekend, they'd have to work whenever they could—even if his mom was around.

Eddie wasn't sure his dad would go for it. But Dad said sure—he'd be over after dinner.

"It'll be dark," Eddie said.

"I'll dig up my old work lamps," Dad said. "Don't sweat it." He hung up. A moment later, Mom came in from work.

"Dad's coming over after supper," Eddie said. "Is that okay?"

Mom pulled off her coat and drummed her fingertips on the kitchen counter. "No," she said.

"What?" Eddie said. "Why not?"

Mom picked up the phone and started to dial. "Because I'm going to invite him over for supper too."

✳ ✳ ✳

Eddie sat down to dinner with his mother and father for the first time in eight years. He thought it would be awkward. He thought no one would have anything to say to each other. He thought there would be a lot of forks scraping across plates and people clearing their throats.

He was right.

Dad coughed and put down his fork. "It's really good," he said.

Mom raised her eyebrows and clucked her tongue. "It's a pre-roasted chicken with frozen peas and powdered mashed potatoes."

"It's still good," Dad said. "I usually grab a ninety-nine-cent cheeseburger at the drive-thru."

"Of course you do," Mom said.

Eddie sat up. He recognized Mom's tone. He kind of wondered why she'd even invited Dad over.

"So," Eddie said, pushing his plate away to signal he was done. "The car's looking pretty good, isn't it, Mom?"

She nodded. "It is. I'm impressed with how quickly you two have gotten so much done."

"He's a natural," Dad said. "Just like his father."

Eddie liked to hear that.

"I don't doubt it," Mom said. She pushed her chair back and stood, grabbing a couple of empty plates as she did. "I'll clean up. You two had better get to work."

"Thanks," Dad said. He winked at Eddie. "It's just like old times, isn't it?"

"Oh yeah," Mom said. "Just like that." She was being sarcastic, Eddie could tell, but she was also smiling.

Eddie stepped back and wiped his greasy hands on a rag. Dad's work lamp hung above the Camaro's open hood.

"Doesn't seem like Mom minds having you around, huh?" Eddie said.

"No," Dad said. He leaned across the engine and tightened a bracket. "I guess not."

"That's good, right?" Eddie said.

Dad looked at him sideways very briefly. "It's not bad," he said. "But listen. Tell me more about this show we're entering."

"Oh, sure," Eddie said, tossing the rag aside. Excited about the race, he pulled the folded-up schedule from his back pocket.

CHAPTER NINE

On Thursday afternoon, all the work under the hood was finished. Dad dropped the lid and said, "What do you say? Do we take it for a spin?"

"Definitely," Eddie said. He headed for the passenger door.

"Whoa, whoa," Dad said. "I'm not driving."

He tossed the keys across the hood, and Eddie caught them. "Seriously?" he said. "Awesome."

The Camaro started like a dragon waking

up in a very bad mood. It growled and roared and coughed. When Eddie revved the engine, a treeful of crows took off to escape the wrath of the beast.

"Sounds good, huh?" Dad said.

"Sounds amazing," Eddie said. He slipped it into first gear, eased off the clutch, and they were off—after two jerky starts and two stalls.

"You'll get used to it," Dad said. "It's not exactly the precise and gentle five-gear stick they tested you on, is it?"

"Not at all," Eddie said. He kept half an eye on the revs as they climbed toward four thousand. He shifted into second.

"Take a left up here," Dad said. "Let's see what she can do on the freeway."

"I don't know," Eddie said. Driving in second on the surface streets was one thing, but really pushing this engine? On the freeway? He'd never done any driving like that before.

"Hey, if you're gonna race this beast in two days, you need to feel how it acts with your foot to the floor."

"I guess," Eddie said.

"Trust me," Dad said. He laughed. "Man, your mom would kill me if she heard me say that."

Eddie swallowed, nervous, but he obeyed. In a few moments, the Camaro was rolling down the interstate entrance ramp. It was more crowded than Eddie had hoped for. He took a few deep breaths, trying to relax.

"Get into the left lane," Dad said. "It'll open up in a mile or so."

Eddie checked his mirror, looked over his shoulder, and slid into the middle lane, then the left.

"Push it a little," Dad said.

Eddie gritted his teeth and pressed hard on the gas pedal. It was heavy. The steering wheel vibrated in his hand. The MPHs climbed and the engine roared.

"Keep pushing," Dad said. "Fourth gear."

The Camaro hit seventy, then eighty.

Eddie quickly checked the revs: they were into the five thousands. "Oh yeah," he said, and quickly stomped the clutch and threw the shifter into fourth. The engine settled into a low rumble.

"Can you hit a hundo?" Dad said, grinning.

"I don't know," Eddie said. "Seems like a bad idea."

"I guess," Dad said with a shrug. Not exactly disappointed but maybe a little. "That's all right. You better grab the next exit. You can drop me at home."

"Oh, okay," Eddie said. He'd have to drive home on his own. That would be a first.

Eddie made it across three lanes of traffic and off the exit for his dad's neighborhood. Dad directed him through the local streets to a housing complex. A sign out front read *Lake Wood Community.*

Eddie pulled to the curb and left the car running in neutral. He chuckled to himself at the name of the apartment complex. There wasn't a lake or a woods anywhere near it.

"Thanks for the ride, man," Dad said, one hand on the door handle.

"Sure," Eddie said. "Thanks for helping so

much with the car."

Dad glanced out the window as he opened the door. Suddenly he slammed it closed again, sinking back into the passenger seat. "Drive," he said, his face suddenly ashen.

"What?" Eddie said, leaning forward, trying to get a look at whatever his dad had seen out the window.

"Just drive!" Dad said.

Eddie, still looking out the passenger window, put the car in first and started to pull away from the curb. It jerked forward and stalled.

"Dammit!" his dad said. "Should I drive?"

"No," Eddie said, starting it up again. As the engine roared to life, a boom sounded against the driver's window.

A man yelled for Eddie to open the door, his face red and wrinkled with anger.

"Drive, Eddie," Dad said. He pushed the gear shift into first. Luckily, Eddie's foot was already on the clutch. Muttering a quick prayer, Eddie slammed the gas and released the clutch. The tires screamed. The engine revved. The Camaro squealed away from the curb, leaving two lines of burnt rubber on the street behind it.

"Who was that?" Eddie said.

"Never mind," Dad said. "Just—just head to your place, I guess."

Eddie checked the rearview mirror. The guy from the window climbed into a little Honda. He was heading after them.

"He's following us," Eddie said.

"Dammit," Dad said, turned halfway around in his seat. "You're gonna have to lose him."

"Are you kidding me?" Eddie said. He turned sharply at the next block and spotted the entrance back onto the freeway. "I've been driving for less than a week!"

"We can't pull over and switch places," Dad said. "He'll be on top of us in no time."

"Who is he?" Eddie said.

"Just get on the freeway and push this baby as hard as you can," Dad said. "If you can make it to your exit, he'll have no idea where we went."

Eddie zoomed up the entrance and nearly clipped a Kia in the right lane. The other driver slammed on the brake, and Eddie just slipped in ahead of him. He got a very rude gesture for his trouble.

"Don't get us killed," Dad said, his voice tense.

"Yeah, I'll do my best," Eddie muttered.

He jerked the wheel hard and slid into the middle lane. He zipped past two sedans and swerved right to pass a tractor-trailer.

"You passing a truck on the right?" his dad shouted. "Are you nuts?"

"I guess so," Eddie said. But he sped up even more, switching back to the middle lane to pass a family in a decrepit station wagon.

"Your exit's coming up," Dad said. "Get back over."

Eddie checked the right. It was clear. The Honda was back there someplace. He just hoped the driver wouldn't spot him exiting.

"I think we're clear," Dad said as they rumbled down Eddie's block. Eddie pulled up in front of his house and cut the ignition.

Dad took a deep breath before forcing a smile and slapping his thigh. "All right," he said. "We're all right."

"What was that all about?" Eddie.

Dad waved it off. "It's nothing," he said. "It's not something you need to worry about." He popped the door and climbed out.

"Where are you going?" Eddie said. "Won't that dude be waiting for you back at your place?"

"I'll find somewhere to crash till it blows over," Dad said.

"Till what blows over?"

"Don't worry about it," Dad said. He closed the door and started to walk toward the bus stop. Eddie ran after him.

"Wait a minute," he said. "Why don't you crash with me and Mom? I'm sure it'll be okay if she knows you're in trouble."

"Don't count on it, man," Dad said. "Besides, it would be weird, and I'll be fine. Okay? You forget about it. Tomorrow we get the paint done and we're ready for the show on Saturday, all right?"

The bus rolled up just as Dad hit the bus stop. With a short wave, he climbed aboard.

CHAPTER TEN

Eddie slept badly that night. He was still full of adrenaline after the car chase. And besides, he knew his dad was in trouble.

It's gotta have something to do with that carburetor, Eddie thought as he got ready for school in the morning. *Something's weird about this whole thing.*

In the school parking lot, Eddie ran into a few of the guys from auto tech. They were standing around a classic Mercury Cougar. It had a fresh paint job: orange with a black stripe up the hood.

"Hey, Eddie," called one of the motorheads. "Got that Camaro running yet?"

"Sure," Eddie said. "Got it up to a hundred on the freeway last night."

"Nice," said another guy, nodding.

"You might have some tough competition," said the guy in the Cougar's driver's seat.

"Right," Eddie said, stepping up to the window. "Because it does the quarter mile in 10.2, right?"

"You heard that?" said the driver, grinning.

"I heard you say so," Eddie said, "but it's bull."

The other auto tech guys laughed, and the Cougar owner opened the door, ready to fight.

"Whoa, whoa," Eddie said, hands in the air. "I'm not looking for trouble."

"You found it anyway," the guy said. He gave Eddie a shove, and one of the other tech kids stepped in.

"Save it for the quarter mile," he said. "All right?"

The Cougar owner backed off. Eddie hitched up his book bag and hurried away.

* * *

"Mom," Eddie said as he came in from school that afternoon. "We gotta get that paint perfect. This other dude at school—"

He stopped short as he stepped into the kitchen. His mom and dad sat together at the table, two cans of beer open in front of them.

"Hi," Eddie said. "Um, hi, Dad."

"Hey, man," Dad said. He stood up. "School good?"

"Sure," Eddie said. He shook the cobwebs from his head and went on. "So a dude in the auto tech school has a Cougar he says does the quarter in ten and a half seconds or something. And it looks real good too."

Dad rubbed his hands together. "Got some competition, huh?" he said. "I ain't worried. We saw what that Camaro could get up to last night, right?"

Eddie froze and he glanced at Mom. She smiled at him. "I don't want to know," she said, getting up. "But I do have this for you."

She grabbed a brochure off the counter

and handed it to Eddie.

"What's this?" he said.

"That's a custom auto paint shop," Dad said. "A friend of your mom's owns it."

"For real?" Eddie said. The glossy, full-color brochure showed off intense custom paint jobs. At the top, it read *Zeph's Body and Paint*.

"His sister works with me at the hospital," Mom said.

Dad coughed and pushed his chair back. "Thanks for the beer," he said. "I guess I better take off."

"What?" Eddie said. "Aren't you going to come with to get the paint job?"

"Nah," he said, putting on his coat. "It's Thursday night—Grudge Night. I thought I'd head up to the drag strip, see if I can't earn back that seven hundo."

He winked and headed for the door.

Mom's friend was waiting in front of his shop

when they got there. He was on the short side and kind of wide. Not fat—more like a short brick wall.

"Hey, Janice," he said as they walked up. Eddie hung back and watched his mom hug the guy. "That's your boy, huh?"

Eddie smirked at him.

"Hey," the guy said, putting out his hand for a shake. "I'm Zeph. You look exactly like your dad, you know that?"

"How do you know my dad?" Eddie said.

Zeph shrugged. "I've known your parents since back in the day," he said. "Your dad and me were in auto tech together."

He wiggled his eyebrows a little and smiled. "I hear you're getting into that, huh?" he said. "That's why we're here, right?"

Without waiting for an answer, he slipped between Eddie and his mom and stepped up to the Camaro, parked at the curb. "Look at this old girl," he said, running a hand over the roof. "The body sure needs a little attention from me, though, doesn't it?"

"That's why we're here, Zeph," said Mom.

"We really appreciate it." She looked at Eddie. "Right?"

"Oh," Eddie said. "Right. Thanks a lot."

"It's no problem," Zeph said. "We're not talking some kind of sick custom job, you understand. Tomorrow, you're not picking up some hot ride with flames down the side."

Mom giggled and Eddie rolled his eyes.

"But I'll knock out the big dents in the body panels," Zeph said as he walked a slow circle around the Camaro. "Throw down a premium sealer. And then a coat of . . . black?" he added, glancing at Eddie.

"Okay," Eddie said.

Zeph nodded and stopped at the grill. "I'll put a white stripe up the hood too," he said, waving his hand over the area like he could make it appear by magic.

"Cool," Eddie said.

"All right," said Zeph. "Come by after school's out tomorrow. Sound good, Janice?"

"Sounds great," Mom said. "Thanks."

Eddie muttered thanks too. Then he turned away and headed for the bus stop.

Mom didn't hurry after him, so he glanced over his shoulder. Mom was giving Zeph a long hug goodbye.

Eddie didn't say a word to his mom the whole ride home.

✳ ✳ ✳

Eddie took the bus straight from school to Zeph's shop the next afternoon. As he walked up to the door, Zeph pushed through it, smiling but confused.

Squinting at the sun behind Eddie, Zeph said, "Hey, kid. I didn't think I'd see you down here. Weren't you happy with the paint job?"

"What?" Eddie said. "I haven't even seen the paint job. I'm here to pick it up."

Zeph nodded and closed his eyes. "Ah, a little miscommunication," he said. "Your dad was here an hour ago. He said you and Janice knew all about it."

Eddie didn't get it. He had never even talked to Dad about picking the car up for him. "Oh, okay," Eddie said. "I mean, right. I forgot.

See ya."

Eddie started for the bus stop.

"You need a ride someplace, kid?" Zeph called after him.

"No," Eddie called back without stopping. He'd take the bus.

CHAPTER ELEVEN

Eddie got off the bus near Dad's apartment complex. He walked down the sidewalk with his hands in the pockets of his hoodie and his head down.

I can't believe he picked up the car without telling me, he thought. *And he told Zeph that me and Mom knew? Why would he lie?*

When he got closer to the Lake Wood Community sign, he heard a familiar sound: the Camaro's big block engine roaring to life.

Eddie ran. The freshly painted Camaro sat at the curb a block up, chugging away—bound to take off at any second.

"Hey!" he shouted. "Dad!"

The engine revved even louder, drowning Eddie out.

He ran faster down the sidewalk, waving his arms. The Camaro pulled away.

"Dad!" he shouted, stopping at the curb. "Stop!" He put his hands on his knees, catching his breath. "Dammit," he muttered.

The Camaro shrieked to a stop at the end of the block, leaving tire tracks behind it. The driver's door popped open, and Dad's head appeared.

"Eddie," he said, flashing a funny grin. "What are you doing here? I was just on my way to your house."

Eddie hurried to the car and climbed into the passenger seat. Dad got back in and they started off.

"I came looking for you," Eddie said, still out of breath from running.

"Oh yeah?" Dad said. He floored the gas pedal and roared onto the freeway toward Eddie's place.

Eddie nodded. "Zeph said you picked up the car," he said.

Dad shrugged and slid into the left lane. Then he pushed the revs up and shifted into fourth gear. The way he was driving, it was almost like he didn't want to hear what Eddie had to say.

"Zeph said you told him that me and Mom sent you to get the car," Eddie went on. "That we knew you'd be getting it instead of us."

"Yeah," Dad said, still smiling. The speedometer was up to 85 MPH. "He wouldn't give me the keys otherwise." He shook his head, like it was no big thing. "I don't know what he thought I was trying to pull. Just doing you a favor."

"Oh," Eddie said. A favor.

Dad guided the Camaro over to the right and then off the freeway. Neither of them spoke until the Camaro was at the curb in front of Eddie's house.

"Thanks," Eddie said as he climbed out. He slammed the door behind him and strode for the house as Mom came out the front door.

"There you are," she said. "When Zeph called and said you'd both come by, I thought—well, I didn't know what to think."

"Just a misunderstanding," Dad said, leaning on the top of the car, still standing with the driver's side door open.

Mom put an arm around Eddie's shoulders. "Everything okay?" she asked Dad.

"Sure," Dad said, smiling. "Why wouldn't it be?"

"Then you're off to the bus stop now?" Mom said.

Eddie glanced at her. She wasn't smiling. Dad's smile faded quickly too, but he recovered quickly and chuckled.

"Of course," he said. He closed the car door and then tossed the keys over the car. Eddie grabbed them from the air.

"I'll see you at the track tomorrow for the race," Dad said. "See ya." He headed up the block toward the bus stop.

As they watched him walk away, Eddie looked at his mom. "What was that all about?"

She kissed his cheek and said, "Don't worry about it. I'm sure it's nothing."

CHAPTER TWELVE

Just south of the city was a huge mall with a huge mall parking ramp and an extra overflow parking lot. During the holiday shopping season, both the ramp and the lot would fill to capacity. But for most of the year, the overflow lot sat unused.

This Saturday, though, the auto tech school had taken it over. It was fenced off, with bleachers set up along both sides. A Christmas tree stood on one end—the drag race starting lights pole. Hanging over the entrance gate was a sign: *Annual High School Drag and Show.*

Eddie pulled in slowly. The Camaro was huge.

Good thing Dad fixed the power steering, Eddie thought as he slid in among the Mustangs, Challengers, Dusters, Firebirds, and GTOs, along with a few other Camaros.

Mom whistled in the passenger seat. "Lots of great cars here," she said. Her voice was quiet and rich, like they were in church or something. "I hope your dad makes it. He'll get a kick out of this."

Eddie pulled up to a woman with a clipboard, one of the auto tech teachers, and rolled down the window.

"Eddie King," he said.

"Camaro SS," she said, smiling. "1969?"

"Yup," said Eddie. "427."

"Nice," she said, running the tip of her pen down the clipboard. "You're in space 17." She pointed to the left. "That way, next to the Cougar."

"Of course," Eddie mumbled. He thanked the teacher, then rolled up the window and pulled into his assigned space. He and Mom climbed out just as Dad reached the front gate.

"Hey," he called over as he handed a five-dollar bill to the teacher manning the pedestrian entrance. Dad hurriedly walked toward them, his head swiveling to check out the other cars. When he reached Eddie and Mom, he said, "Can you believe they made me pay the spectator fee?"

Eddie was about to reply, but Dad was too excited. He kept on talking. "Boy, the Camaro has never looked so good," he said, running his hand over the tail. "Old Zeph did a great job with the paint," he added, looking at Mom.

"He sure did," she said without smiling.

A whistle blew, and the teacher with the clipboard waved her arms from the bleachers nearby.

"Hood open, people," she said. "Show's starting."

Dad clapped his hands and rubbed them together, grinning like a wolf. "I'm going to walk around," he said. "I'm too nervous to just stand here. Besides, there's lots of muscle to check out."

Eddie and Mom watched Dad walk off.

"I'll take a seat in the bleachers," she said. She squeezed Eddie's shoulder and headed off. He popped the trunk and leaned on the driver's door to wait for the judges.

There were three of them in total. Two were teachers from the auto tech school, and the third wore a black jacket with gold writing on the back: *Eat My Dust Magazine.*

"Who's that guy?" Eddie called across the top of the Camaro.

The Cougar owner sneered at him. "Tom Hart," he said. "He runs an online magazine about muscle cars. He's the guest judge this year."

"Oh," Eddie said.

"And last year," the Cougar owner said. "And the year before that. And before that . . ."

Eddie laughed.

"Camaro looks good," the other guy said. "Who did the paint?"

"Zeph," Eddie said. "Know him?"

The other guy nodded. "Anyway, good luck," he said. "Here they come."

The judging lasted an hour overall. The three judges looked at each car inside and out, under the hood and inside the trunk. Tom Hart asked Eddie to start his engine up and give it some revs. The teachers asked Eddie what kind of work he'd done.

"Looks real good," Tom Hart said when he was done with the Camaro. Then he moved on to the Cougar. He said, "Looks real good," after checking out the Cougar too.

"Glad that's over," the Cougar owner said. "Finally, we get to race."

CHAPTER THIRTEEN

"You ready for this?" Dad asked Eddie as he pulled on his helmet—a required safety precaution.

"Not really," Eddie said. "You saw me stall this thing like five times, right?"

Dad chuckled. "You'll do fine," he said. "Just don't waste your power on the start. No spins. No squeals. Just go!" He chopped at the air, like his hand was a muscle car.

"No problem," Eddie said, but it was. And in his first race, he was up against that Cougar—of course.

He got in and closed the door, took a few deep breaths, and rolled up to the start line. He kept his eyes on the Christmas tree, waiting for that steady amber light to tell him he and the Cougar were lined up and ready.

The top lights lit up. Eddie heard the Cougar rev. He tried to match it.

The second lights lit up. Eddie's clutch foot tingled.

The third set of ambers lit up. He held his breath.

Green. Eddie pulled off the clutch and the brake. The tires shrieked as he lurched over the start line. In the other lane, the Cougar screamed down the track, well ahead. The driver had gotten a better start—much better—which meant he'd won.

The race was over in thirteen seconds. The Cougar crossed the finish line. Eddie crossed two seconds later. He slowed and stopped and banged the steering wheel.

Eddie looked over at the Cougar. The driver flashed a thumbs-up, so Eddie flashed one back.

Dad and Mom waited for him to climb out on the sidelines.

"Disappointed?" Mom asked.

"Not really," Eddie said, pulling off his helmet. "First race and all that. No big deal."

"Nah," Dad said, mussing Eddie's hair. "No big deal at all."

"What happens now?" Mom asked.

"I think we have lunch," Eddie said. "I better get the Camaro back to space 17 first, though."

"You and Mom go eat," Dad said. "I'll park it up. Any excuse to take the old beast for a quick spin—even one under twenty MPH."

"Thanks," Eddie said as he gave Dad the keys. Mom flashed a tight-lipped smile, and they went to grab a couple of burgers as Dad climbed into the Camaro.

☀ ☀ ☀

Dad never showed up at the cookout area. When Eddie and Mom had finished their burgers and chips, they cleaned up and headed for the parking area. Space 17 was empty.

Mom ran for the teacher with the clipboard. "Hey!" she shouted, frantic. "Did someone drive off with the Camaro SS?"

"The '69?" the teacher said. She glanced at her clipboard. "Oh, right. Just before lunch. All checked out."

"You let him leave?" Eddie said. "Didn't you remember I drove it in?"

"Look," the teacher said. "There are a lot of cars here today and lots of drivers. I can't remember everyone. But he showed me his ID," she added quickly as Eddie and his mom started to interrupt her. "And he showed me the title. It was his car."

Eddie's jaw dropped. Mom went right on ranting, but Eddie didn't listen. It didn't matter, because the teacher was right. It was Dad's car, and it always had been.

CHAPTER FOURTEEN

The bus ride was quiet. When Eddie and Mom got home, she went inside, but Eddie didn't. He transferred to a different bus and rode it for nearly an hour to Lake Wood Community.

"Are you sure you want to go over there?" Mom had asked before Eddie climbed on the next bus. "He's not going to give the car back, sweetie. I know your father well. Too well."

"I know," Eddie said as he flashed his pass at the driver. "I just need to talk to him."

The doors closed with a *hiss* and a *thwack*.

⁑ ⁑ ⁑

"I figured you'd turn up," Dad said as he let Eddie into his apartment.

It was small and bright but dusty. It smelled like socks and bacon and dirty laundry.

"I'm sorry to take off like that," Dad said. He dropped onto the couch and looked at a college football game on the TV. "I knew you wouldn't understand."

"Then explain," Eddie said, standing next to the TV.

Dad didn't look at him. "It's my car," he said. "It's always been my car. I bought it. My name's on the title." He scoffed. "And let's be honest. I did most of the work to get it running so well again."

"Thanks," Eddie said.

Dad sighed and clicked off the TV. "Look, it was nice hooking up with you again," Dad said, finally looking at Eddie. "You're a cool kid. If you want to get into cars, you'll do fine. But it's my car, not yours."

"So you just took it," Eddie said.

"Listen, I need the money," Dad said. "That carburetor wasn't—let's just say it wasn't 100 percent on the level. I have people to pay back. I have gambling debts. I have real, grown-up stuff to deal with. All you gotta worry about is passing math. Know what I mean?"

Eddie didn't answer.

Dad groaned as he stood up and opened the apartment door, inviting Eddie to leave.

"Then this was never about me at all," Eddie said. "You didn't care about seeing me again. You just figured if the Camaro got fixed up, you could sell it, make some more money to flush down the toilet."

"Come on," Dad said. "I admit, it was cool to see you and connect. And I love the old car. I even enjoyed working on it with you—you think I would've dropped seven hundo on that carb if I didn't think it was worth it?"

Eddie shrugged.

"But it wasn't real," Dad said, moving away from the door toward the fridge. He pulled out a can of beer and cracked it open. "I'm not getting back with your mom, right? I'm not going to suddenly become some kind of father figure for you after ten years of being on my own and doing my own thing."

"I guess," Eddie said.

"Look, you wouldn't want me around for long anyway," Dad said. "Trust me."

He took a long swig of his beer. While the can was still at his lips, Eddie stepped out. He left the apartment door open.

* * *

"Disappointed?" Mom said as Eddie stepped through the front door.

"I don't know," he said, dropping onto the couch.

Mom sidled up next to him. "You don't know?"

Eddie shrugged. "I never really believed he was back. I mean, back for good."

"But you hoped so anyway?" she said.

"A little," Eddie admitted. "But that's not what's really disappointing."

"No?"

Eddie shook his head. "Dad's disappointing," he explained, "and part of me is him."

"True," Mom said. "Your dad has some not-so-nice qualities."

"Which means I do too."

Mom patted his knee. "Maybe. But your father has some good qualities too." She stood up. "And you've got those too. So focus on the good."

Mom headed into the kitchen, and Eddie heard the water run at the sink. He leaned his head back and looked at the ceiling.

"Good qualities," he muttered to himself. Then he called into the kitchen as the water turned off. "What would you think of my switching to the auto tech school?"

Mom stuck her head through the kitchen door. "I'd love it," she said, smiling.

Eddie smiled too. He'd focus on the good.

THE CHEVY CAMARO

MODEL HISTORY

The Chevy Camaro was unveiled in 1966 and
entered production in 1967. General Motors
(GM) hoped its everyday practicality and sports
car performance would make the Camaro a
hit with drivers. Nicknamed a "pony car," the

Chevy Camaro joined a group of automobiles known for their affordability, compact size, and performance. Muscle car collectors still pine after the original 1967 model.

While no one is certain where the name *Camaro* came from, Chevrolet managers have said that a Camaro is "a small, vicious animal that eats Mustangs." Available as a two-door car (coupe or convertible), the Chevy Camaro could be equipped with either a straight-six engine, rated at 140 horsepower, or a V8 engine.

The first generation Camaro offered three different specialized packages. These included the **RS**, **SS**, and the **Z/28**. The RS had the fanciest appearance; it featured a bright trim on the outside and headlights that would pop up only when in use. The SS package was performance-focused. It had a larger V8 engine than the original as well as superior handling. The **Z/28** was a performance package designed specifically for racing.

In 1975, the Chevy Camaro gained attention at the International Race of Champions (IROC) series. From 1975–1980 and 1984–1989, in twelve seasons of competition, the Chevy Camaro won twelve titles at this race.

SIGNATURE MOVES

A rear-drive pony car, the Camaro is able to "drift" easily when handled by a skilled driver. (Drifting is the act of sliding through a corner by "oversteering"—turning more sharply than necessary—at the beginning of a turn so much that the rear wheels lose traction.)

The Camaro is also known for its ability to "ski." Skiing is the act of driving a car while it is balanced on only two wheels. In order to get a car into this position, drivers often will drive two wheels up to a higher surface (such as a ramp) or, if the car has a high center of gravity, the driver might turn sharply to get it into position.

THE CAMARO ON FILM

The Transformers series features the Chevy Camaro in the form of the popular character Bumblebee. Perhaps one of the most famous "skiing" stunts occurred in the 2007 *Transformers* film. Bumblebee ejects two characters and then skis past them.

THE CAMARO TODAY

Between 1966 and 2002, Chevrolet produced four generations of Camaros. Production stopped following the 2002 model (the 35th anniversary edition). For model year 2010, however, a fifth-generation Camaro was produced. This generation is still in production. Its "retro" makeup is based on the first generation models of the Camaro.

Released in model year 2013, the Chevy Camaro NASCAR is a race car model. It debuted at Daytona in 2013.

EDDIE'S CAMARO

ENGINE: 430 horsepower V8 engine, high displacement (427 cubic inches) big-block, overhead valve train with two valves per cylinder (six total)—revs to 8,000 RPM; 450 horsepower carburetor; gaskets, seals, O-rings, clamps, bolts and nuts replaced with brand new parts (low-cost, but necessary fixes); new V-belt installed

DRIVETRAIN: chopped down the manual shifter (making it into a "short shifter" reduces the time it takes to change from one gear to another—better acceleration)

SUSPENSION: Guldstrand mod—raises the roll center of the car and increases camber by relocating the upper arm's mounting point; front sway bar; rear sway bar; steering tie-rods (they were worn after years of racing behind 'em! These pieces of metal attach your steering wheel to the strut, which makes your wheels turn. Very important!)

BRAKES: front and rear brake pads (for better friction—brake pads have to be in good shape

get a car going over 100 mph to stop); front
and rear brake lines (the Camaro's been sitting
around for so long that the old ones were
rusted!); front calipers

WHEELS/TIRES: lightweight wheels; rims (they
improve handling and make the Camaro look
like a professional racecar!)

EXTERIOR: body dents knocked out; painted with
premium sealer and shiny black paint; white
racing stripe up the hood; tightened brackets;
replaced front and back bumper with more
recent Camaro bumpers; new headlights;
window tint; front spoiler (not only does it
look awesome, it also provides increased
downforce which enhances tire traction—the
Camaro will be hugging the curves with ease!);
restored and cleaned the vintage SS badging

INTERIOR: heavy gas pedal makes for easier
acceleration; 4-speed shifter and clutch;
superior handling steering wheel; floor mats to
keep the dirt and snow off the cabin carpeting

ELECTRONICS: ignition coils; fuel level sensor

(the old one was whacky—it jumped from full to empty with no warning!); a new speaker system to pump some tunes before the start of a race

Check out the rest of the
TURBOCHARGED series:

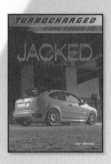

LOOK FOR THESE
TITLES FROM THE

TRAVEL TEAM

COLLECTION.

SOUTHSIDE HIGH

ARE YOU A SURVIVOR?

The Alliance

Bad Deal

Beaten

Benito Runs

Dance Team

Deadly Drive

The Fight

Full Impact

Overexposed

Plan B

Recruited

Shattered Star

Check out all the books in the

SURVIVING · SOUTH SIDE

collection